Hansel and Gretel

First published in the UK in 2005 by Mercury Junior
An imprint of Mercury Books
20 Bloomsbury Street, London WC1B 3JH

This book was conceived, edited and designed by
McRae Books Srl
Borgo Santa Croce, 8,
50122 Florence, Italy
info@mcraebooks.com

Project Director: Anne McRae
Design Director: Marco Nardi
Text: Elizabeth McLeod
Illustrations: Maria Mantovani, Renzo Barsotti
Layout & Editing: McRae Books
Cover design: Open Door Ltd

Color separations: R.A.F., Florence
Printed and bound in China

Title: Hansel & Gretel
ISBN: 1 904668 61 5

Hansel and Gretel

Illustrators
Maria Mantovani & Renzo Barsotti

Mercury
Junior

Once upon a time a woodcutter and his wife lived with their two children near a big, dark wood. The little boy was called Hansel and the little girl Gretel. Their mother died when they were small and their father remarried.

Then there was a famine and the woodcutter did not know how to feed his family. "What will become of us? How can we feed our children, when we haven't enough for ourselves?" he asked his wife.

"Husband," she said, "we'll take the children into the woods and leave them there. They'll never find their way home." "My poor children!" cried the woodcutter, "I can't leave them to die in the woods." But in the end his wife convinced him.

Hansel and Gretel, who could not sleep for hunger, overheard what their stepmother said. They were frightened. Hansel crept outside and filled his pockets with shiny white pebbles.

The next morning the stepmother woke the children early and they all set off for the woods. Gretel's apron held two small slices of bread and Hansel's pocket was bulging with pebbles.

Every few steps Hansel turned and dropped a pebble on the path behind him.

They came to the middle of the woods and the woodcutter made a fire so they would not be cold. The stepmother said, "Now children, lie down by the fire and rest until we come to take you home." The children ate their bread and soon fell fast asleep.

When they woke up it was dark. Little Gretel began to cry. "How shall we find our way home?" she cried. But Hansel knew that they only had to wait for the moon to come up, and then the moonlight would show them the trail of pebbles that would lead them home. After a long time, they arrived home safe and sound, but it was well past midnight!

The children's father was overjoyed to have them back. But soon another famine came and the stepmother wanted to get rid of the children once and for all. "We'll take them even deeper into the woods," she said. Her husband was forced to agree.

Early next morning they set off again. This time Hansel crumbled the bread his stepmother had given him and dropped crumbs behind him, so that they would be able to find their way home.

Just as before, the children were left by a fire in the middle of the woods and they slept until dark.

But when the moon came up, they discovered that the birds had eaten the trail of breadcrumbs. They were lost! They wandered through the forest all night and all the next day, and the day after, and the day after that.

On the third morning they came to a clearing in the woods. There stood a lovely cottage made entirely of bread and cake and all kinds of sweets. Hansel and Gretel shouted for joy.

"Eat this!" said Hansel, handing his sister a slice of chocolate cake window sill, as he busily ripped a piece of candy off the roof for himself.

Just then a very old woman came out of the cottage. "Ah, you dear little things," she said, "eat all you want and then come inside to sleep. You can live with me now." At first the old woman was kind to the children. But she was really a wicked witch and she planned to cook them and eat them up as soon as they were fat enough.

She locked Hansel in a cage and made Gretel take him lots of food to fatten him up. But Gretel was given almost nothing to eat.

One morning the wicked old witch decided it was time to boil Hansel up for lunch. She told Gretel to bring water for the pot and to make a fire under it. While the water was boiling, she told Gretel to climb into the oven to see if it was hot enough to bake some bread. But what she really wanted to do was slam the door behind her and cook her as well!

Little Gretel pretended she could not get into the oven. The old witch scolded her saying, "Stupid! Look how easy it is. Even I can do it!" As she clambered into the oven, Gretel gave her a huge shove and slammed the door shut.

"Hansel! Hansel!" she shouted, "we are saved! The wicked old witch is dead." She opened the cage and Hansel jumped out and hugged his sister. They both danced for joy.

Before they left the witch's house they filled their pockets and Gretel's apron with all the precious stones and gold she had collected over the years. Then they set off for home.

When they had walked for two hours they came to a big lake. There was no bridge and no boat, and the children did not know how to cross it. Then they saw a big white duck. They jumped onto its back and it took them quickly across the lake.

They walked for a little while longer and then they came to a well-known road. At long last they saw their father's house in the distance. They began to run.

They found their father alone in the house. His wife had died. He had been very sad since he left the children in the woods. The children hugged and kissed him. Then they showed him the treasure they had taken from the witch's house. And they all lived happily ever after!

Series titles:

Snow White and the Seven Dwarfs

Cinderella

Puss in Boots

Sleeping Beauty

Beauty and the Beast

Little Red Riding Hood

Thumbelina

The Ugly Duckling

Hansel and Gretel

Town Mouse and Country Mouse

The Three Little Pigs

Pinocchio